COLORADO

OKLAHOMA

Hesperus Peak

Blanca Peak

ck

Jicarilla Apache

Farmington

San Juan

Taos

Picuris

San Ildefonso

Santa Clara

Pojoaque

Tesuque

Nambe

Conchiti

Santa Fe

Jemez

Santo Domingo

Santa Ana

San Felipe

Mount Taylor

Zia

Sandia

Fort Sumner

Laguna

Albuquerque

Acoma

Isleta

NEW MEXICO

ni

Rio Grande

Mescalero Apache

N

W

E

S

TEXAS

To my mother, Nancy H. Warren.

The author would like to thank David Kozak and Gary Matlock—both of the Fort Lewis College Anthropology Department—for their expertise in checking the manuscript for accuracy. He would also like to thank Toh-Atin Gallery and Thompson River Trade Company, both of Durango, Colorado, for allowing him to photograph artwork from their collections.

Book design by Christine Cuccia and Vandy Ritter.

Typeset in Oz Handicraft, Weiss and Syntax.
Printed in Hong Kong.

Library of Congress
Cataloging-in-Publication Data
Warren, Scott S.
     Desert Dwellers / by Scott S. Warren.
     p.   cm.
     ISBN: 0-8118-0534-4
     1. Indians of North America—Southwest, New—Social life and customs.
     I. Title
     E78.S7W35   1997   96-28679
     979'.00497—dc20   CIP   AC

Distributed in Canada by Raincoast Books
8680 Cambie Street, Vancouver, British Columbia V6P 6M9

10 9 8 7 6 5 4 3 2 1

Chronicle Books
85 Second Street
San Francisco, California 94105
Website: www.chronbooks.com

Front Cover Photo: clockwise from upper left: Taos Pueblo, New Mexico; Zuni Olla Maidens at the Gallup Inter-Tribal Ceremonial, Gallup, New Mexico; Saguaro cacti and Baboquivari Peak, Tohono O'odham Nation, Arizona; Navajo barrel racer at a rodeo in Mexican Water, Arizona.
Title Page Photo: Hopi Butterfly Dance.
Back Cover Photo: Drummers at a Hopi dance performed at an art show in Sedona, Arizona.

Desert Dwellers

Native People of the American Southwest

Written and Photographed by Scott S. Warren

chronicle books san francisco

Monument Valley
lies at the heart
of the vast
Navajo Nation.

CONTENTS

The Cochise Stronghold is believed to be where famed Apache leader, Cochise, is buried.

THE FIRST SOUTHWESTERNERS

The American Southwest is a beautiful yet harsh land. Redrock mesas and lofty mountains tower above dry desert. Rivers flow through deep canyons. Temperatures climb above 100 degrees in the summer and dip well below freezing in the winter. Rain may not fall for months at a time, or it may send flash floods crashing down dry stream beds. For countless centuries this fascinating and often forbidding region has been home to many different groups of American Indians. And, many American Indians still live in the Southwest now. They enjoy all of today's conveniences, yet they also follow traditions which date back to the earliest days of their ancestors existence.

The history of the American Indians of the Southwest began thousands of years ago. Anthropologists—those scientists who study people and their cultures—believe that American Indians first migrated to North America from Asia during the last Ice Age 15,000 to 40,000 years ago, crossing over a land bridge that connected Siberia with Alaska. The earliest people to live in the Southwest roamed the region over 10,000 years ago. At first they hunted woolly mammoths and other large animals. When these prehistoric animals became extinct, the early Southwest Indians continued to hunt smaller game, such as bison and deer, and they gathered wild plants. Eventually, these hunter-gatherers learned to grow corn and other food. They also learned how to make pottery. Having adopted new ways of life, these prehistoric Southwesterners evolved into four different groups: the Anasazi, the Hohokom,

Indian Pottery

It is thought that pottery was first introduced to the American Southwest from Mesoamerica (what is now Mexico) more than 2,000 years ago. These Maricopa pots, like most Indian pottery of the Southwest, were formed by hand.

Dance at Santa Clara Pueblo in New Mexico.

the Mogollon, and the Patayan.

Beginning 2,000 years ago, these four groups started growing their own food. They built cities of stone. They were skillful artists and they had complex religious ceremonies. For reasons which are still not fully understood, however, these groups began to change or disappear soon after 1100 a.d. Some groups moved to new parts of the Southwest while others migrated in from outside the region. By the time the first European explorers visited the Southwest in 1540, many native civilizations had already come and gone. But the American Indians living in the Southwest today are, for the most part, descendants of those who lived there thousands of years ago.

By studying both the past and the present, anthropologists have learned much about the complex and rich lives of native Southwesterners. Many of their traditions were greatly influenced by the natural environment in which they lived. In places where water was available, for example, farming—rather than hunting and gathering—became a primary source of food. This, in turn, led to the development of ceremonies performed to bring rainfall and abundant crops. And permanent villages were built near farmable lands so that the people could tend their crops.

In places where no rivers or streams flowed, or where the top-soil was poor, hunting game and gathering wild plants offered better sources of food. Knowledge about wild animals and plants was important, as was the need to move from place to place during the year to harvest different wild foods. In these ways and others, each group developed customs and beliefs suited to the land on which they lived.

Early Southwestern Indians borrowed ideas from one another, as well as from American Indians living outside the Southwest. They were also influenced by European settlers who moved into the region after 1540. The Navajos, for instance, learned many things from the Pueblo people. Apache groups borrowed ideas from the Plains Indians who lived to the east. And after 1540, many Southwestern Indians adopted new ways of life from Spanish and Anglo-American settlers.

Because of their enduring strength, the Indians of the Southwest have been able to preserve many of their traditional beliefs and customs. Many tribes still perform ancient religious ceremonies and rituals. Ancient stories are told and retold. Native languages are spoken. Traditional arts are passed down from generation to generation. Native foods are prepared and traditional homes are built.

Of course, the American Indians of the Southwest have adapted to the contemporary world as well. In doing so, they live fascinating lives that blend ancient traditions with today's conveniences. While a Pueblo boy rides his bike with friends one day, the next day he may be dancing with his elders in the plaza. And, after completing her Sunrise Ceremony, an Apache girl is soon back in math class learning about algebra. ❖

Stories In Stone

Although anthropologists do not know the meanings of most pictographs (painted on the stone) and petroglyphs (carved into the stone) created by the early Southwesterners, they do know that this Navajo pictograph in Arizona's Canyon de Chelly marks the passage of Spanish Conquistadors through Navajo territory.

The Pueblo

Corn Dance

Performed by most eastern pueblos, the Corn Dance usually takes place in the spring or summer, and may include hundreds of dancers of all ages. Children often participate but they must practice many hours before the dance. Like many pueblo ceremonies, the Corn Dance is performed to bring rain and a plentiful harvest.

According to the Pueblo (pwe-blo) Indians' creation myth, their ancestors once lived in three dark underworlds. Searching for light, they climbed a spruce tree into this world. When they emerged, the Pueblo people were taught how to survive in their new land. For each Pueblo group this sacred place of emergence—called the Sipapu (see-pa-poo)—is one of the most important places in their traditional world. The idea that their ancestors emerged from the ground reflects the Pueblo people's belief that all life—plants, animals, and people—begins with the earth.

The Pueblo Indians are the descendants of the Anasazi (an-a-sa-zee), who lived in the region we now call the Four Corners (Utah, Colorado, New Mexico, and Arizona) between 100 b.c. and 1300 a.d. The early Pueblo Indians were skilled farmers who grew corn, squash, beans, and cotton. They hunted deer, bison, rabbits, and other game and they gathered wild plants as well.

Although each Pueblo group has its own name for itself, the word pueblo—Spanish for city or town—was first used in 1540 by the Spanish explorer Francisco Vasquez de Coronado. Coronado had heard tales of cities of gold, and he traveled north from Mexico with a large army to search for riches. What he found instead were earthen villages that looked golden at sunset. Coronado's visit marked the first recorded contact between the native peoples of the Southwest and European explorers.

In the decades following Coronado's expedition, the Spanish enslaved the peaceful Pueblo Indians and punished them for fol-

Most pueblos
are one or two
stories high but
Taos Pueblo is
four stories tall.

7

New Mexico's Nineteen

New Mexico's nineteen pueblos are spread out across the northern and western parts of the state. Those located to the east along the Rio Grande are often referred to as the eastern pueblos and those scattered among the arid mesas to the west are the western pueblos. The eastern pueblos include Taos, Picuris, San Juan, Santa Clara, San Ildefonso, Nambe, Pojoaque, Tesuque, Cochiti, San Felipe, Santo Domingo, Santa Ana, Zia, Jemez, Sandia, and Isleta. The western pueblos are Laguna, Acoma, and Zuni.

lowing their traditional religion instead of Christianity. In 1680, however, the Pueblo people united and overthrew the Spanish in what is known as the Pueblo Revolt. Considered to be the most successful American Indian rebellion in North American history, the Pueblo Revolt forced the Spanish to leave the Southwest. In 1692 the Spanish once again conquered the Pueblos. But after their return, the Spanish treated the Pueblo people more fairly.

Like those built centuries ago, today's Pueblo villages consist of connected homes that are similar to apartment buildings. These homes are made out of stone blocks or adobe bricks, and plastered with mud. Most pueblos are located in valleys near rivers or streams, but one—Acoma Pueblo—sits atop an isolated mesa that towers 365 feet high. Each pueblo features one or more plazas. As the center of Pueblo life, plazas are where ceremonial dances are held. Pueblos also have one or more kivas (key-vaz), or chambers, where certain religious ceremonies and gatherings occur. Some Pueblo kivas are underground; others are aboveground. Some are round and others are square.

While all Pueblo groups share certain cultural traits, there are some differences as well. One of the most striking is language. Among New Mexico's nineteen Pueblos, five different languages are spoken. Although some words may be similar from one Pueblo language to the next, speakers of these different languages cannot always understand each other. Today, many Pueblo Indians speak their traditional language as well as English.

Along with differences in language, there are also differences in how Pueblo communities are organized. The Eastern Pueblos are divided into two groups which anthropologists call moieties (moy-ih-tees). These two groups may include the Summer and Winter moieties, North and South moieties or Turquoise and

Squash moieties. Each moiety usually has its own kiva and is often responsible for certain ceremonies. The Winter moiety, for example, performs those dances which take place in the fall and winter, while the Summer moiety conducts those which occur in the spring or summer.

The Western Pueblos (Acoma, Laguna, and Zuni) are divided into several different clans, such as the Eagle, Sun, Antelope, Snake, Bear, Water, and Turkey clans. In these pueblos, children are born into their mothers' clans and husbands join the clan of their wives. Like moieties, clans have ceremonial functions and they help strengthen family relationships within the community.

Most Pueblos have

Buffalo Dance at San Ildefonso Pueblo.

Puye Cliff Dwellings were occupied by the ancestors of the Santa Clara Pueblo people.

two forms of government: one they have traditionally followed and one that was introduced by the Spanish in the early 1600s. In traditional Pueblo government a religious leader known as a cacique (kay-see-kay) directs both the religious activities and many of the daily affairs of the village. The cacique is considered to be the spiritual father of his people and he usually holds his position for life. The cacique is assisted by war captains. Although war captains were traditionally responsible for conducting warfare, they now help direct ceremonies, and are often in charge of tribal lands.

Each Pueblo also has a governor, a position established by the Spanish centuries ago. Some Pueblo governors are elected; others are appointed by the cacique. Governors typically deal with outside authorities, like the state and federal governments.

As it has been for many centuries, religion is very important to the Pueblo Indians. However, there is no word for religion in any of the Pueblo languages. That is because the Pueblo people do not separate religion from their everyday lives. Pueblo religion is based on the idea that all people must live in harmony with the universe. The most important way to maintain this harmony is to perform certain ceremonies throughout the year. Some of these ceremonies are privately conducted by religious leaders inside the kivas, but others unfold on the plazas in spectacular dance. These dances also serve as prayers for rain, plentiful harvests, successful hunts, and the well-being of all.

The Corn Dance is performed by most eastern pueblos. It usually takes place in the spring or summer, and may include hundreds of dancers of all ages. The dancers wear branches of evergreen which symbolize things that grow. Girls and women also wear colorful headdresses, or tablitas (tab-lee-tas), which are often decorated with cloud symbols. Dancers shake gourd rattles to imitate the sound of rain, and the beating of drums represents the heartbeat of the earth. By performing the Corn Dance, the members of the Pueblo hope to ensure that the rains will fall and the harvests will be plentiful.

Other ceremonies, such as the Deer Dance and Buffalo Dance, honor an animal's spirit and help ensure a successful hunt. In these ceremonies the dancers dress as the animal and copy its movements. Because hunting is traditionally a wintertime activity, animal dances usually occur in the winter. These ceremonies may involve only a few dancers, or as many as several dozen.

An important ceremony that takes place in November or December at the Zuni Pueblo is the Shalako (sha-la-koe) Ceremony, a night-long dance that includes ten-foot-high masked

Pueblo Christianity

The first Spanish to visit the Southwest mistreated the Pueblo people and tried to keep them from practicing their own religion. After the Pueblo revolt of 1680, however, the pueblo people eventually accepted Christianity alongside their traditional beliefs. Today, all of New Mexico's nineteen pueblos include a Catholic church.

Santa Clara Pueblo potter, Toni Roller, forms a pot by hand out of coils of clay.

figures known as Shalakos. Shalakos are considered to be messengers of the Rain Gods, so this dance serves as a prayer for rain. In addition, because it is believed that the spirits of the dead return to the village at this time of the year, the ceremony is thought to reunite the Zunis with their ancestors. As with many other Pueblo dances, feasts of chile stew and bread baked in hornos (outdoor ovens) are provided during the Shalako Ceremony.

Just as Pueblo religious beliefs and ceremonies date back many centuries, Pueblo arts are also based on very old traditions. Pottery was first introduced to the American Southwest from Mesoamerica (what is now Mexico) more than 2000 years ago, and Pueblo artists still hand-form their pots from coils of clay. Once the pot is smoothed with a polishing stone, it may be painted with designs and then hardened in an outdoor fire.

Another traditional craft practiced by Pueblo artists is jewelry making. The prehistoric ancestors of the Pueblo people made beads, pendants, and earrings out of a beautiful sky-blue stone called turquoise, which they believed brought good fortune to those who wore it. After learning how to work with silver in the 1800s, Pueblo artists began making jewelry out of turquoise and silver.

Because Pueblo pottery, jewelry, and other craft items are prized by collectors from around the world, traditional arts provide a good income for many Pueblo Indians. More and more, Pueblo children are learning these time-honored artistic skills from their parents. Still other Pueblo Indians work outside of the pueblo as government officials, doctors, university professors, and in other jobs.

Along with their contemporary lives, many Pueblo people still hold traditional beliefs which reflect their deep and abiding respect for the world around them. One Taos Pueblo explains his people this way: "We have lived upon this land from days beyond history's records, far past any living memory, deep into the time of legend. The story of my people and the story of this place are one single story. No man can think of us without thinking of this place. We are always joined together." ❖

A hornos, or outdoor oven made of adobe, at Acoma Pueblo.

THE HOPI

The Color Of Corn

The Hopi have grown a variety of corn for thousands of years and each color has a special meaning. White symbolizes the east and purity. Red corn represents the south and respect. Blue symbolizes the west and patience. Yellow represents north and knowledge.

Although corn has long been important to American Indians throughout North America, to the Hopi (ho-pee) Indians it is the very essence of life. Corn has sustained the Hopis in their desert homeland for countless centuries, and it plays an important role in both everyday Hopi life and in Hopi ceremonies.

Dancers hold ears of corn during many Hopi ceremonies. Cornmeal is used to bless and purify, and to make offerings to the spiritual world. Before a Hopi couple gets married the bride goes to the house of the groom's mother where she grinds corn for three days. And when a Hopi child is born, a perfectly formed ear of white corn is placed in the crib next to the child. Representing Mother Earth, the ear is used to bless the child during a naming ceremony on the twentieth day of the child's life.

The Hopi live in twelve villages nestled among three mesas in northeastern Arizona. Some villages are perched on top of the mesas while others are located just below. Similar to Pueblo villages, most Hopi villages feature connected homes arranged around outdoor plazas. Hopi villages also include kivas where religious ceremonies are performed. The oldest Hopi village, Oraibi (oh-rye-bee), dates back to 1100 a.d. and is thought to be the oldest continually inhabited community in the United States.

Like the Pueblo Indians, the Hopi are descendants of the prehistoric Anasazi. But, unlike the Pueblo groups who mostly migrated to the Rio Grande Valley in what is now New Mexico, the Hopi stayed in the arid Four Corners area. The Hopi do not

In the Hopi
Butterfly Dance
young Hopi
women wear
colorful tablitas.

Dry Land Farmers

Considered to be some of the best dry land farmers in the world, the Hopi still grow their corn and other crops without irrigation water, just as they have for many centuries. By planting their fields near springs or in washes which occasionally flood, by using special varieties of seeds which do well in arid climates, and by performing many sacred ceremonies, the Hopi have adopted quite well to farming in their desert environment.

call their ancestors "Anasazi." Instead, they refer to them as the Hisatsinom (hee-sat-see-nom), or the "Ancient People."

While the Pueblo Indians speak different languages, all Hopis speak the Hopi language. Today, all Hopis speak English, but most also speak the Hopi language as well.

Traditionally, each Hopi village was independent from the others, and each village had its own chief, or kikmongwi (kik-mon-gwee). Today each Hopi village is still governed by a village chief, but most are also represented in a tribal council. The council deals with matters of concern to all Hopis, such as relations with the federal government and tribal land use.

Hopi society is divided into several different clans, such as the Bear, Snake, Spider, and Eagle clans. Children become members of their mother's clan and husbands join that of their wives. Clans are important because they bring unity and structure to Hopi society. Clan members work together to grow corn for the entire clan and they all help in raising children.

The Hopi have long relied on farming as their main source of food. The Hopi still grow their crops much in the same way their ancestors did. Tractors may be used to plow larger fields, but no irrigation water is used. Because the Hopi live far from any rivers or streams, they have learned special ways to grow food in a very arid land. Some fields are planted near springs, while others are planted in arroyos (uh-roy-ohs), or dry stream beds, which flood after summer showers. The Hopi have also developed plants that are better adapted to a dry climate. While corn is their main crop, the Hopis also grow beans, squash, and some fruits.

According to Hopi tradition, their ancestors lived in three different underworlds before emerging into this one, the Fourth World. The Hopi's place of emergence, or Sipapu, is located in the

Grand Canyon. Upon reaching the Fourth World, the Hopi clans migrated in four directions before they arrived at the mesas where they live today. When they came to these mesas, each clan had to demonstrate that they could make it rain by performing a ceremony. If the clan was successful, they settled and their ceremony was then added to the Hopi calendar of ceremonies. This coming together of the Hopi people is known as the gathering of the clans.

Today, the Hopi people still perform many of the ceremonies that were traditionally performed during the gathering of the clans. Because water has always been important to the survival of the Hopi people, many of their ceremonies are performed to bring rain. These ceremonies are also believed to bring harmony and

Betatakin Cliff Dwelling, located near Kayenta, Arizona, was home to the ancestors of the Hopi.

17

Hopi dancers perform
in Sedona, Arizona.

well-being to all. Hopi ceremonies begin inside the kivas and
involve many hours of private rituals such as singing, building of
altars, and praying. The ceremonies last several days and end with
a public dance in the plaza. The yearly cycle of ceremonies is
divided into two six-month periods. One period starts soon after
the winter solstice (usually in January) and continues to summer.
All ceremonies held during this time involve masked dancers
known as kachinas (ka-chee-nuz).

Kachinas are the spirits of plants, animals, natural forces (like
wind and lightning), and the ancestors of the Hopis themselves.
Kachinas carry the Hopi's prayers for rain, fertility, and good
health to the spiritual world.

Kachina dances feature Hopi dancers who dress up as the kachina
spirits. These dancers wear fanciful masks, their bodies are often
painted, and they wear turquoise jewelry. Many kachina dancers

also wear evergreen boughs and eagle feathers. The first kachina dance is the Winter Solstice Ceremony, which takes place when the days begin to grow longer. It marks the start of preparations for the upcoming planting season. Prayers are made for the well-being of family, friends, animals, and even cars, trucks, and tractors.

In February, the Bean Dance occurs. It begins with the planting of beans in the kivas to help bring good harvests later in the year. Near the end of this nine-day ceremony, kachina dancers distribute the bean sprouts to the villagers. The Bean Dance is especially important to Hopi boys and girls around the age of eleven because during this ceremony they are initiated into kachina societies. With this initiation, Hopi boys and girls start to carry out ceremonial duties that will last for the rest of their lives.

Also in February, monster-like Ogre kachinas arrive in some of the Hopi villages. Going from house to house, Ogre kachinas help get younger children to behave by threatening to take them away. Parents can "save" their child by offering food to the Ogre kachinas and promising that their child will behave.

In April, as the days become longer and warmer, the kachina dances move from inside the kivas to the plazas. An interesting feature of many plaza dances are the sacred Hopi clowns. Often painted with white stripes, Hopi clowns make fun of Hopis and non-Hopis alike by staging funny acts. The clowns make spectators laugh, but their gestures are also serious because they point out the weaknesses of humankind.

The Going Home Ceremony, or Niman (nee-man) marks the end of the kachinas' stay in the Hopi villages. Niman begins after the summer solstice, and lasts for sixteen days. Only on the last day, however, does a public dance take place in the plaza. The dancers give kachina dolls to young Hopi girls, so that they may

Kachina Home

For half the year the kachinas are believed to live among the Hopi villages. But in summer, after the Niman, or Going Home Ceremony, these helpful spirits return to their home high in the San Francisco Peaks near Flagstaff, Arizona, carrying the Hopi's prayers for rain with them.

Noted carver, Neil David, creates a kachina doll out of the wood of a cottonwood tree root.

learn about the many different kachina spirits, and they give toy bows and arrows, rattles, and games to Hopi boys.

During the six months following the kachinas' departure, several non-kachina dances take place. Perhaps the best known is the Snake Dance. In this ceremony, specially trained dancers carry live snakes—some of which are poisonous—in their hands and mouths while prayers for rain are offered. At the end of the dance the snakes are released in the desert so that they may take the Hopi's prayers for rain to underground spirits.

Another dance that takes place while the kachinas are away is the Butterfly Dance. In this dance, young, unmarried Hopi women wear colorful tablitas and dance alongside young Hopi men. September and October bring women's society ceremonies, or Basket Dances. Basket Dances are performed to cure illnesses, and to help bring fertility and good harvests to the people. Finely woven baskets, along with other gifts, are thrown to the spectators during these dances.

Just as traditional ceremonies are still an important aspect of modern Hopi life, so too are a variety of traditional arts that date back hundreds, even thousands of years. Among them is basket making. Some Hopi baskets are made from the straight leaves of the yucca (yuk-ka), a plant that is common in the desert. Other Hopi baskets are woven together from willows and rabbit brush stems. Hopi baskets are prized by collectors because of the beautiful designs that are woven into each one. The Hopi themselves use baskets in ceremonies, weddings, and everyday life.

Hopi potters today create distinctive pots and bowls using ancient pottery techniques. Like Pueblo potters, Hopis form their pots by hand from coils of clay, then they fire them in outdoor fires. Detailed designs in different colors are painted onto the finished pots with paintbrushes made from yucca leaves. Some Hopi designs are geometric, while others depict birds or other animals.

Hopi silversmiths are known for their silver overlay technique. By joining two layers of silver—one with a design cut through it and the other with a blackened surface—Hopis create beautiful rings, bracelets, belt buckles and earrings.

Perhaps the most distinctive of all Hopi creations are kachina dolls which are carefully carved from the roots of cottonwood trees. Over time, kachina dolls have become very detailed and fanciful, and more and more non-Hopis buy them for their artistic beauty.

Besides their artistry, many other things link today's Hopis with their prehistoric past. While they could easily buy all of their food at the grocery store, many still grow corn just as their ancestors have for centuries. Many Hopis spend a lot of their time preparing for and performing religious ceremonies, even though they also hold full-time jobs. And Hopi children—while they attend modern schools, watch videos, and ride bicycles, just like kids all over the United States—participate in a variety of vibrant ceremonies. In these and many other ways the Hopi people are successfully blending their rich traditional heritage with the conveniences and demands of the contemporary world. ❖

Kachina Doll

Originally created to teach Hopi children about the many different kachinas, kachina dolls are now also created for sale to collectors from around the world. Taking many hours to complete, the best kachina dolls will bring skillful Hopi carvers thousands of dollars for each one.

THE TOHONO O'ODHAM AND THE PIMA

Man In The Maze

To the Tohono O'odham and Pima peoples, the Man in the Maze symbol is very important. The human figure represents humankind and the circular maze represents life itself. Just like life, the maze is filled with many paths. The Man in the Maze symbol is often woven into baskets by artisans from both groups.

Towering above the desert near Tucson, Arizona, is a jagged mountain called Baboquivari (baa-bo-key-var-ee) Peak. This mountain is nearly 8,000 feet high and is visible for many miles. For the Tohono O'odham (toe-hoe-no oh-oh-dom) Indians, however, Baboquivari Peak is much more than a landmark. According to their traditional beliefs, it is home to Elder Brother, or I'itoi (ee-ih-toy). From this prominent mountain Elder Brother watches over the Tohono O'odham, or "People of the Desert."

The Tohono O'odham, along with the closely related Pima (pee-ma) Indians, are the two largest groups of American Indians living in southern Arizona. The Tohono O'odham live mostly in the three-million-acre Tohono O'odham Nation—the second largest American Indian reservation in the United States. Most Pima Indians live on smaller reservations near Phoenix.

Archaeologists are not certain about where or how the Tohono O'odham and Pima Indians originated. One theory suggests that they descended from the prehistoric Hohokam (ho-ho-kom) people. The Hohokam were farmers who lived in what is now southern Arizona between 300 b.c. and 1400 a.d. Another theory suggests that the Tohono O'odham and Pima Indians migrated north from Mexico after the Hohokam civilization faded.

Because the Tohono O'odham and Pima peoples both speak the Pima language, and because they share many traditions and beliefs, they are sometimes thought of as a single group. But having traditionally lived in two different desert environments, they

Saguaro cacti
and Baboquivari
Peak in the
Tohono O'odham
Nation.

A Tohono O'odham woman harvests saguaro cactus fruit in Saguaro National Park, Arizona.

originally followed two different ways of life.

In order to survive in a vast desert with no rivers, the Tohono O'odham traditionally lived in two different villages during the year. In summer when rains were more frequent, the Tohono O'odham moved to "field villages," which were located along desert washes. Because these washes occasionally flooded, the Tohono O'odham were able to plant fields of corn, squash, and beans.

After the rainy season ended and all of their crops were harvested, the Tohono O'odham moved to their "well villages," which were located near springs in the mountain foothills. They hunted deer, desert bighorn sheep and other game. And they gathered hundreds of different wild plants, including grass seeds, mesquite (mess-keet) beans, and the fruit of the saguaro (sa-war-oh) cactus. The Tohono O'odham used long sticks to knock the fruit off the tops of the tall cactus, and they turned the sweet red fruit into syrup and ceremonial wine. Today, some Tohono O'odham still harvest the fruit of the saguaro in the traditional way.

Tohono O'odham girls play the traditional game of toka during a school tournament at Sells, Arizona.

In contrast to the two-village system of the Tohono O'odham, the Pima Indians traditionally lived in larger, permanent villages along the Gila (hee-la) River, near where the city of Phoenix is now located. Like the Hohokam who once inhabited this area, the Pima Indians used river water to irrigate large fields of corn, squash, beans, and cotton. The Pima people also harvested mesquite beans and other wild foods. In the 1870s the Pima's agricultural way of life came to an abrupt end, however, as Anglo-American farmers upstream used much of the water in the Gila River to irrigate their own fields. The river dried up, leaving the Pimas without water to grow food. In order to survive, the Pima Indians had to give up their traditional farming lifestyle to work in nearby cities.

While the Tohono O'odham and Pima peoples originally lived in different environments, other aspects of their traditional worlds were similar. The Tohono O'odham and Pima peoples both built round, flat-topped homes out of branches, thatched grass, and mud plaster. A ramada (ra-ma-da)—a roof made of branches and grass— was constructed near the homes to provide shade for cooking and

San Xavier

Today most Tohono O'odham are followers of the Catholic religion. Their introduction to Christianity dates back to 1687 when the Spanish missionary, Father Eusebio Kino, first ventured into their homeland. Father Kino established several missions, the largest of which is the San Xavier (san ha-veer) Mission located on the Tohono O'odham Nation.

shelter for sleeping in the summertime. In the late 1800s, the Tohono O'odham and Pima peoples began building rectangular homes with walls made of mud packed between two layers of saguaro cactus ribs. These structures were called sandwich houses. Today, most Tohono O'odham and Pima Indians live in contemporary homes and wells make it possible for them to live in communities throughout their desert homeland.

Before the advent of modern wells, the Tohono O'odham and Pima peoples often performed ceremonies to bring rain to their desert lands. The Wine Ceremony was one of the most common ceremonies performed by the Tohono O'odham. After the saguaro cactus fruit was harvested, a wine was made from the juices of the fruit. It was then consumed by adults in the village as they recited prayers to summon the rain clouds. Today, the Wine Ceremony is still performed in a few villages.

Just as some traditional beliefs and practices have survived in contemporary times, so too has the traditional Tohono O'odham and Pima artistry of basket making. Carefully woven from yucca, beargrass, and devil's claw, Tohono O'odham and Pima baskets were originally used for harvesting and storing food.

Another tradition still practiced by both the Tohono O'odham and Pima peoples is a game called toka (toe-ka). Similar to field hockey, this sport is played by girls using sticks cut from mesquite branches. The idea is to knock the "ball" (two pieces of wood tied together) across the opponent's goal line and then to pick it up. Toka is often played by school teams in organized tournaments.

While some Tohono O'odham and Pima traditions are many centuries old, one that dates back only to the late 1800s is waila (why-la), or chicken scratch music. Waila blends Mexican folk music and German polka music (from German immigrants who settled nearby in the 1800s) and combines the sounds of accordions, saxophones, drums, guitars, and fiddles. The name chicken scratch refers to the sound that dancing feet make on dirt floors.

Within the last few centuries other Indian groups have moved into southern Arizona. During the 1600s, the Maricopa (mare-ih-co-pa) Indians migrated east from the Colorado River and settled alongside the Pima Indians. Having been forced out by neighboring Quechan (keh-chan) and Mohave (mo-ha-vee) Indians, the Maricopa are descendants of the prehistoric Patayan (pa-ta-yan) people. And during the 1800s, thousands of Yaqui (ya-key) Indians moved north from Mexico and resettled near Tucson and Phoenix. The Yaqui people still perform their Deer Dance, and they conduct colorful Easter ceremonies.

Although the Tohono O'odham, Pima, Maricopa, and Yaqui peoples no longer rely on the desert environment for their survival, they still remember the old ways and they continue to hold a deep respect for their bountiful desert homeland. A Tohono O'odham man once said: "All year round we were watching where the wild things grew so we could pick them. Elder Brother planted those things for us. He told us where they are and how to cook them. Those are the good foods." ❖

Tohono O'odham dancers carry likenesses of clouds in a parade at the O'odham Tash Festival, Casa Grande, Arizona.

27

THE PAI

Yucca

The resourceful Pai utilized many parts of the yucca plant which grows throughout their traditional territories. The yucca fruit was roasted in pits and then stored for eating later in the year. The plant's spiky leaves were made into cord, or thin rope. And yucca roots were used to make soap.

The Pai (pie) Indians include three related Indian groups: the Yavapai (yav-a-pie), Hualapai (hoo-wa-la-pie), and Havasupai (hav-a-su-pie). The Pai once lived across a large area of what is now western, central, and northern Arizona. Today, they mostly live on tribal lands scattered across Arizona. The word Pai means "people" in their native Yuman language.

Although the Pai, especially the Havasupai, farmed a little, all three groups mostly relied on wild plants and animals to survive. While not as hot and dry as the desert lands of southern Arizona, Pai territory was still quite arid. This meant that they had to move from place to place throughout the year depending on where plants grew and when they ripened. Their hunting and gathering lifestyle was similar to that of earlier Indian groups who lived in the Southwest thousands of years ago.

The Hualapai and the Yavapai also relied mostly on hunting and gathering to survive. Tubers (plants with edible roots) such as wild garlic and wild potatoes were dug up in the winter. In the spring, leafy plants such as wild spinach were gathered, as was the century plant, or agave (a-gah-vey). In the summer, cactus fruits, mesquite seeds, and other desert plants offered additional sources of food for the Pai. And autumn was the best time of year for gathering acorns, pinyon nuts, walnuts, sunflowers, grass seeds, juniper berries, and the fruit of the yucca. Roasted and dried, yucca fruit was stored for use later in the year. Yucca leaves were made into cord, or thin rope, which was then woven into mats, baskets, and

200-foot high Mooney Falls along Cataract Creek on the Havasupai Reservation.

The village of Supai along Cataract Creek on the Havasupai Reservation.

other useful items. Yucca roots were also used to make soap.

While the Yavapai, or the "People of the Sun," and the Huala-pai, or the "Pine Tree People," moved from place to place all year long, the Havasupai, or the "People of the Blue-Green Water," (named after the mineralized water of Cataract Creek which flows through their homeland in the Grand Canyon) did traditionally live in one place for part of the year. In the fall and winter, the Havasupai moved from camp to camp on the mesa tops of their territory where they gathered wild food and hunted game. In the spring, however, they returned to Cataract Canyon where they grew corn, squash, and beans. It is believed that the Havasupai learned some farming practices from the Hopis.

Throughout the year, the Pai hunted a variety of animals, including rabbits, deer, antelope, bighorn sheep, and several types of birds. When hunting in large groups, Pai hunters drove their prey into pens or nets. When hunting alone, they often camouflaged themselves by wearing deer-head masks. They also used traps and snares to catch small birds and mammals. Older boys and men did most of the hunting while girls and women usually gathered wild plants.

Because the Pai moved around a lot, traditional Pai homes were simple and easy to build. Summertime shelters often consisted of brush lean-tos, or wickiups (wik-ee-ups), which provided shade from the hot sun. In the winter the Pai lived in larger, dome-shaped houses made from pole frames and thatched grass or juniper bark roofs. Mud-plastered structures were also built, as were brush ramadas for shade.

Perhaps because the Pai were mostly hunters and gatherers, they were not as concerned with bringing rain to their homelands. Instead, most of their religious ceremonies served to cure illnesses. Performed by medicine men, or shamans, Pai healing ceremonies included singing over the patient and symbolically sucking out objects which were believed to be causing the patient harm. The Havasupai, who were more involved in farming than the Hualapai and Yavapai, did perform some rain and harvest dances. Again, it is thought that the Havasupai may have adopted these ceremonies from the Hopi.

Although the early Hualapai, Havasupai, and Yavapai did make some pottery, the most important Pai handicraft was basket making. Using different techniques and materials, Pai women created a variety of basketry items. Burden baskets were made for carrying firewood and other large loads. Cone-shaped baskets

Havasupai Hoopsters

Although Supai is located 8 miles from the nearest road, the village has all the necessities. There is a store, restaurant, church, hotel, post office, and school. Havasupai kids growing up in Supai are seldom bored because they can visit the nearby waterfalls, go horseback riding, and even play basketball whenever they want.

31

were made for collecting seeds and wild foods. Some baskets were made for storing food, and still others were used to carry water. These were made waterproof by smearing pine sap or boiled agave juice over them. Today, Hualapai, Havasupai, and Yavapai women still create basketry which is known for its beautiful designs and fine workmanship.

Because the Pai groups ranged over such a large portion of the Southwest they often came in conflict with Anglo American settlers during the 1800s. After being placed on a reservation in 1871, the Yavapai were soon forced to move again to live with the Apache. The Yavapai were eventually granted their own reservation in the early part of this century. The Hualapais fought a fierce war with the United States Army in the 1860s. After loosing the war, the Hualapais were forced to settle with the Mojave people in nearby California. In 1883 the Hualapai were granted 900,000 acres that is today known as the Hualapai Reservation. And the Havasupai lost all but 500 acres of their territory to Anglo-American miners and ranchers who encroached on their lands in the late 1800s. In 1975, after several years of legal battles, Congress added another 160,000 acres to their reservation.

Although their traditional lifestyles have been mostly replaced by grocery

Pai basket makers are renowned for the high quality of their work.

stores, cars, and homes, today's Pai Indians have managed to hold on to pieces of their traditional world. Some Havasupai still farm along Cataract Creek. Pai craftspersons still make fine basketry. Some Hualapai and Havasupai still revere Spirit Mountain in nearby Nevada as the place where mankind was created, and some Yavapai still think of Montezuma Well (a limestone sinkhole in central Arizona) as the place where the first people emerged into this world. During a congressional hearing concerning the expansion of the Havasupai Reservation, former tribal chairman, Lee Marshall, said, "I heard all you people talking about the Grand Canyon. Well, you are looking at it. I am the Grand Canyon." ❖

The foot trail to Supai follows Hualapai Canyon to Cataract Creek, Havasupai Reservation.

THE NAVAJO

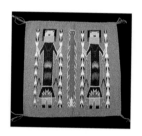

Navajo Rug

According to Navajo tradition, the Navajo people learned how to weave from Spider Woman, an important Navajo deity. Today, Navajo weavers still follow weaving techniques which are hundreds of years old. Totally made by hand, a Navajo rug may take months to complete. While some rugs include geometric designs, others, such as the one above, depict spiritual beings known as Yei.

With great skill and patience, a Navajo (nah-vah-hoe) weaver passes a piece of yarn through threads strung tightly across her loom. She tamps it into place with a wooden comb and then picks up another piece of yarn. It, too, is threaded into the strands and then tamped snugly into place. By repeating this process over and over, the weaver slowly creates a beautiful Navajo rug.

Following traditional Navajo weaving techniques, the yarns used in Navajo weavings are made by hand. First, the wool is sheared from the family's sheep. It is carded to straighten the fibers, and then it is spun into yarn. Lastly, it is dyed with natural dyes. Boiled walnut shells make yellow, ground up onion skins make green, and crushed lichen makes pinkish-orange yarn. This was the way Navajo weavers learned to weave long ago, and it is how they weave today.

With a population of over 200,000, the Navajo are one of the largest American Indian tribes in the United States. Most Navajos live on the 17.5 million-acre Navajo Nation, which stretches across parts of Arizona, New Mexico, and Utah. The Navajo Nation is the size of West Virginia and it is the largest Indian reservation in the United States. According to Navajo tradition, their homeland is defined by four sacred mountains—Mount Taylor to the south, Hesperus Peak to the north, Blanca Peak to the east, and the San Francisco Peaks to the west. These four mountains are still revered by the Navajo people.

Navajo barrel racer at a rodeo in Mexican Water, Arizona.

Although their traditions date back many centuries, the
Navajo are relative newcomers to the Southwest. Anthropologists
tell us that Navajo and the Apache Indians migrated to the Southwest from northern Canada sometime between 1300 and 1500 a.d.
The Navajo and Apache speak a similar language, so it is thought
that they may have once been a single group. It is believed that
they split in two around the time they reached the Southwest.

The Navajo first settled in what is now northwestern New
Mexico, where they came in contact with Pueblo Indians. Anthropologists believe that the early Navajo learned many things from
the Pueblo people, including how to grow crops. After the Pueblo
Revolt of 1680, some Pueblo Indians came to live with the Navajo
to escape Spanish attacks, and because of this the Navajo also
learned about pottery making, and masked dances.

Eventually, the Navajo expanded their territory to include what
is now the Four Corners region. Because this part of the Southwest
was far from early Spanish settlements, the Navajo did not at first

have much conflict with European settlers. But that changed as the Europeans began settling more land in the 1700s. Even though they were occasionally fighting the Spanish during this time, the Navajo people acquired domesticated sheep from them. The Navajo continued to grow crops and gather wild food, but sheep soon became the mainstay of Navajo life. Sheep became an important source of food for the Navajo and also provided wool for weaving. Today, sheep are still important to many Navajo, and flocks of sheep are common throughout the Navajo Nation.

When the United States won the New Mexican territory from Mexico in 1848, the government promised to stop the conflict with the Navajos. Over the next several years, however, they had little success. To end the continued disputes, in 1863 the United States Army ordered Colonel Kit Carson to remove all Navajos from their homelands. After destroying their homes and killing their sheep, Carson and his troops rounded up over 8,000 Navajos and forced them to march nearly 300 miles to Fort Sumner in eastern New Mexico. This march became known as the Long Walk. After four years of harsh imprisonment at Fort Sumner, the Navajo people were finally allowed to return home. By that time, thousands of Navajos had died.

Although the Long Walk is still a painful part of American history, the Navajo people nevertheless proudly served the United States government in more recent times. During World War II, American forces could not relay radio messages without the Japanese intercepting them. To foil the Japanese, the Marines enlisted Navajo men (known as Codetalkers) to send and receive messages in the Navajo language which the Japanese could not understand.

Despite the many changes in their lives, the Navajo people still follow many of their traditional customs. Clan relationships,

Codetalkers

During World War II, American forces could not relay radio messages without the Japanese intercepting them. To foil the Japanese, the Marines enlisted Navajo men to send and receive messages in the Navajo language which the Japanese could not understand. Known as Codetalkers, these Navajo men greatly contributed to the United States' efforts during the war.

Sand Paintings

As part of many Navajo ceremonies Navajo singers spend many hours creating intricate sand paintings. Made from colored sand, cornmeal, and pollen these beautiful images must be cleaned away by sunrise. Today, Navajo artists create smaller sand paintings which are glued into place for sale to collectors.

for instance, are still very important to the Navajo. The Navajo base their kinship on the mother's clan. Mothers are treated with great respect, and older women are often the head of the extended family. Children are born into their mother's clan, and—until recently—couples settled next to the home of the wife's mother after they married. There are more than sixty Navajo clans, and they are still the backbone of Navajo society.

Traditionally, the Navajo settled in small, widely scattered clusters of homes that were occupied by members of the same family. The traditional Navajo home is called a hogan (hoe-gon). Hogans are round or octagonal in shape. They are usually built out of logs, some have domed roofs covered with dirt and hogan doors always face east toward the rising sun. Today, many Navajos live in contemporary rectangular homes, but some still live in traditional hogans.

According to the Navajo creation story the hogan was originally used by First Man and First Woman. First Man and First Woman were two of many spiritual beings known as the Holy People, or Yei (yay). The Holy People lived in several underworlds before they emerged in this world. When they reached this world, First Man and First Woman raised an orphan baby they found on top of a mesa. Her name was Changing Woman. As one of the most important Holy People, Changing Woman created the Earth Surface People, or the Navajo themselves.

Interwoven into all aspects of traditional Navajo life, Navajo religion is based on the idea that the universe contains harmony and beauty. But, when this harmony and beauty is disturbed, misfortune and sickness results. Contact with certain animals such as snakes and coyotes can cause an imbalance, as can lightning and ghosts. To bring harmony and beauty back into the world, Navajo religious men, known as singers, perform a variety of ceremonies.

The most important of all Navajo ceremonies is the Blessingway. To bring good fortune to newborn children, a new home, or perhaps a returning soldier, the Blessingway retells the Navajo creation story through songs, prayers, and sand paintings.

The Navajos also have ceremonies to help heal a sick person. At one time they had more than fifty different curing ceremonies in all. Because Navajo ceremonies are very long and intricate it may take an apprentice singer many years to learn them. Although some of these ceremonies no longer take place, many are still performed regularly throughout the Navajo

A Navajo woman cooking frybread over an open fire in the Carrizo Mountains, Arizona.

Navajo weaver, Marie Begay, at work in her home in Burnham, New Mexico.

Nation. One of these curing ceremonies, the Nightway, lasts for nine days and it only takes place during colder months, when snakes are hibernating and "thunder sleeps." On the last evening of the Nightway, masked dancers dress up as the Holy People. This final dance is often called a Yeibichai (yay-beh-chay).

Traditional Navajo arts are also widely practiced today. The Navajo are best known for their skills as weavers. Collectors often pay thousands of dollars for Navajo rugs, and the rugs may take months to complete. In the past 100 years, Anglo-American traders across the Navajo Nation have suggested designs to the weavers who regularly visited their trading posts and, over time, regional styles have developed. The Ganado style, for example, which arose from the Ganado Trading Post in Arizona, features beautiful red colors.

Besides weaving, the Navajo are also well known as silversmiths. They learned the skill from Mexican silversmiths in the mid-1800s. Soon Navajo craftsmen developed their own designs, which often include beautiful polished pieces of turquoise. Turquoise has special meaning for the Navajo, who believe it represents harmony and beauty. Navajo silversmiths make necklaces, rings, earrings, belt buckles, bracelets, pendants, and pins.

The Navajo also make a variety of baskets for both everyday and ceremonial use. Trays were traditionally used to hold food and for winnowing grasses and grains. Deeper gathering baskets were used when collecting wild food such as pinyon pine nuts. Still other baskets were used in ceremonies such as weddings. Navajo baskets are usually black and red in color. They are noted for their fine quality and beautiful designs and they are widely collected.

Today, many Navajo work in coal mines within the Navajo Nation. Others attend universities to become doctors, lawyers, and other professionals. The Navajo tribe owns a large farm in New Mexico, and tourism is an important Navajo industry. At the same time, the Navajo have managed to hold onto many of their traditions. Through their respect for tradition and their acceptance of the contemporary world, the Navajo are maintaining harmony in their universe. They are following the opening words of the Nightway Ceremony: "In beauty, I walk. With beauty before me, I walk. With beauty behind me, I walk. With beauty above me, I walk. With beauty all around me, I walk." ❖

Trading With the Navajo

Within the past 100 years, Anglo-American traders established trading posts among the Navajo. Trading posts allowed Navajo weavers to sell their weavings, or trade them for food and supplies. The traders often suggested new designs and colors to the weavers and regional styles soon developed. The Ganado style, which arose from the Ganado Trading Post in Arizona, features beautiful red colors.

THE APACHE

Changing Woman

With a piece of seashell hanging on her forehead, Apache girls embody the spirit of Changing Woman during the Sunrise Ceremony. As the first woman on Earth, Changing Woman is the most important of all Apache deities. The Apache people's respect for Changing Woman also reflects the importance that women still hold in Apache society.

Facing the rising sun, a 12-year-old Apache (ah-pah-chee) girl steps in time to the beat of drums and the singing of a medicine man and his helpers. In her hand she holds a cane. It symbolizes the strength that she will need when she becomes an old woman. Hanging on her forehead is a piece of shell. It represents Changing Woman, the first woman on Earth. Known as the Sunrise Ceremony, this Apache ritual prepares the girl for the rigors of growing up.

An important event in the lives of many Apache girls, the Sunrise Ceremony lasts for four days. Members of her family, her friends, and neighbors come to help her celebrate entry into womanhood. At first she dances standing up. Then she kneels down and sways from side to side. After this, she lays on her stomach while her sponsor—an older woman who is a friend of the family—massages her arms and legs to make her strong. On the final day of the ceremony, the girl sits on the ground while she is painted with a mixture of pollen and other natural materials. This gooey mixture is believed to give the young Apache woman the strength of the earth.

The most important of all Apache rituals, the Sunrise Ceremony is still performed by the four Apache groups of the Southwest. These groups include: the Western Apache who mostly live in east-central Arizona; the Jicarilla (hick-or-ee-a) Apache who live in north-central New Mexico; the Mescalero (mess-kah-leer-o) Apache who live in south-central New Mexico; and the Chiricahua

Wickiups at the Apache Cultural Center in Whiteriver, Arizona.

Runners at the
Jicarilla Apache foot
race near Dulce,
New Mexico.

(chair-ih-cow-wah) Apache, who mostly live with the Mescalero
Apache in New Mexico.

Anthropologists believe that the Apache, along with the
Navajo, migrated to the Southwest from northern Canada between
500 and 700 years ago. After reaching the Southwest, the Apache
eventually moved into different areas where they developed different lifestyles and traditions. These differences led to the
establishment of the different Apache groups. Each group's culture
was influenced by the environment in which they lived and by
neighboring Indian groups. Despite their differences in lifestyles
and beliefs, all four groups shared many characteristics.

Traditionally, the Apache were hunters and gatherers. This meant that they often moved from place to place to take advantage of different sources of food. In mountainous areas the Apache gathered pinyon pine nuts, cattail roots, acorns, and grass seeds, among other food items. And in the desert areas they gathered cactus fruits, mesquite beans, and agave plants. After digging up the core of the agave plant, the Apache then roasted it in large cooking pits for two days.

In addition to having great knowledge about wild plants, the Apache were also skilled hunters. When hunting in large groups they often chased the animals to one place where they could then be killed. Other times Apache hunters wore deer or antelope heads and hides so that they could sneak up on their prey. While all Apache groups hunted deer, antelope, and rabbits, the Jicarilla and Mescalero Apache also hunted bison on the plains which bordered their homelands.

Although all Apache groups relied mostly on wild plants and animals for food, the Jicarilla and Western Apache occasionally planted small gardens of corn, beans, and squash. As with the Navajo, it is believed that these Apache groups learned about agriculture from their Pueblo neighbors.

Often on the move, the Apache lived in simple homes that were easy to set up and take down. Known as wickiups, these homes consisted of a dome or cone-shaped frame of poles covered with brush or grass. A smoke hole was left in the middle of the roof for ventilation. In addition to wickiups, the Jicarilla and Mescalero Apache also constructed tipis out of long poles and animal skins.

The Apache people traditionally lived in small family groups that were based on the women's clans. Several family groups, in

Blooming Agave

Like other Indian groups of the Southwest, the Apache relied heavily on the agave, or century plant, which grows many years before blooming. When it finally does it quickly grows a tall stalk and then dies. The Apache waited to harvest it until it flowered because that was when it was most nutritious. After digging up the core of the plant, the Apache then roasted it in large cooking pits for two days.

turn, made up local groups which had their own hunting and gathering areas. These local groups each had a leader who led the group in warfare and the moving of camps. Among the Western Apache, local groups, in turn, were loosely grouped together to form bands.

While traditional Jicarilla Apache society included family groups, local groups, and bands, it was also divided into two large groups: the Olleros (oh-lear-ohs) and the Llaneros (yah-near-ohs). The Olleros represent the sun and animals while the Llaneros represent the moon and plants. These two groups are still recognized by the Jicarilla Apache today, and the tribe holds a foot race between them every September. If the Olleros win the race, the coming year will bring good hunting, and if the Llaneros win, then there will be a long growing season.

Although each of the four Apache groups has their own myths and stories, many aspects of the Apache creation story are shared by all. This story tells of how the first people emerged into this world from an underworld. At the time of their emergence, life on earth was difficult because of monsters which stalked the land. A young maiden named Changing Woman became pregnant by Sun and gave birth to Child Born of Water and Killer of Enemies. These two hero gods eventually made the world safe for the Apache by slaying the monsters. Central to the Sunrise Ceremony today, Changing Woman is still an important deity among the Apache.

Other important spiritual beings in traditional Apache beliefs include the Mountain Spirits, or Gaan (gahn). Unique to the Apache, Gaan are helpful deities who live in the mountains. Often performing at night as part of Sunrise Ceremonies, Gaan dancers wear masks and impressive wooden crowns.

In addition to the Sunrise Ceremony, other Apache rituals were traditionally performed to cure illnesses. The Apache believe

Apache Baskets

Because the Apache moved around a lot, they had little use for breakable pots. Instead, baskets woven from yucca, beargrass, and other plants were fashioned to collect and store food, and for carrying water. Today Apache craftspersons still make baskets for use in ceremonies and to sell to collectors. Often, they feature beautiful designs and many are fringed with buckskin.

A young Apache girl is painted during a Sunrise Ceremony at Whiteriver, Arizona.

that the world is filled with supernatural power which can be harnessed by a medicine man during healing ceremonies. Often lasting for four nights, Apache healing ceremonies include the reciting of prayers, singing of songs, a performance by Gaan dancers, and blessings with pollen. Representing life, pollen is an important part of all Apache ceremonies.

Because the Apache traditionally moved around a lot they had little use for clay pots which might break during their travels. Instead, woven baskets were used to collect and store food, and for carrying water. Today, baskets are still used in Apache ceremonies, and they are also sold to collectors. Some Apache baskets feature geometric designs, while others are decorated with human or animal figures. Many Apache baskets are also fringed with buckskin.

While the Apache mostly relied on hunting and gathering for their survival, they also obtained some goods by raiding their neigh-

Apache Gaan dancers at the O'odham Tash Festival, Casa Grande, Arizona.

bors. Practiced by many early Indian groups, raiding was not meant to kill their enemies. Rather, it was simply meant to get needed items. Spanish settlers were a frequent target of such raids. And, when the United States took control of the Southwest in the mid-1800s and many settlers moved into Apache territory, conflicts continued. Of all the Apache groups that fought the United States Army, the Chiricahua Apache put up the fiercest defense of their homeland.

Under the leadership of Cochise (coe-chees), the Chiricahua Apache fought the United States Army until a treaty was signed in 1872. It promised land for the Chiricahuas, but, after Cochise died in 1874, the reservation was abolished and the Chiricahuas were forced to resettle with other Apache groups. Eventually, bands of Chiricahuas left the reservation against the wishes of the government. One of these bands was led by the Apache medicine man, Geronimo (jere-on-i-moe). For five years Geronimo and his followers eluded the Army. After surrendering in 1886, Geronimo was sent to prison in Florida and the Chiricahua people were disbanded to reservations in other parts of the country.

Despite years of conflict with the United States Army, the Apache still hold on to many of their traditions. Apache women make their livings by weaving fine baskets. The Sunrise Ceremony is still widely practiced as are other ceremonial events. The Apache language is spoken by many. And, while hunting and gathering has been replaced by contemporary lifestyles, the Apache rely on the environment in a different way. All Apache reservations have successful livestock and logging operations, and two Apache reservations own ski resorts.

While many Apache people today make good livings from the natural environment, most also greatly revere the lands which have nurtured them since their arrival in the South-west centuries ago. Echoing the importance of the land to the Apache, Geronimo once said of his homeland: "It is my land, my home, my father's land. I want to spend my last days there, and be buried among those mountains." ❖

The strange rock formations of Chiricahua National Monument served as a hideout for Geronimo and his band of Apache fighters.

49

Visiting Indians of the Southwest

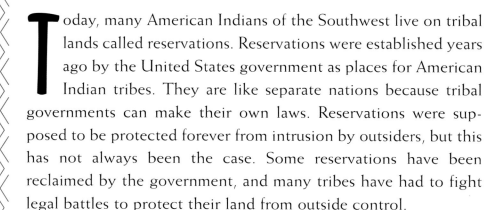

Visiting Reservations

While a visit to a reservation today may reveal some of the problems American Indians face, it can also offer a fascinating look into the traditional lives of Native American peoples.

Today, many American Indians of the Southwest live on tribal lands called reservations. Reservations were established years ago by the United States government as places for American Indian tribes. They are like separate nations because tribal governments can make their own laws. Reservations were supposed to be protected forever from intrusion by outsiders, but this has not always been the case. Some reservations have been reclaimed by the government, and many tribes have had to fight legal battles to protect their land from outside control.

American Indians of the Southwest greatly value their reservation lands. These lands provide jobs through industries such as timber harvesting and tourism. But more importantly, because these reservations are a part of the people's traditional homeland, they provide a vital link to each group's traditional way of life. As it has always been, the earth is still highly respected by the traditional American Indians of the Southwest.

The American Indians of the Southwest have long had to fight to protect their homelands and livelihoods, and they are still facing many problems today. Some tribes are still battling for water rights which were promised years ago. Jobs are in short supply on some reservations, health problems are a big concern, and many Indians live in poverty. The Southwestern tribes are working hard to solve these problems.

While a visit to a reservation today may reveal some of the problems American Indians face, it can also offer a fascinating look into the traditional lives of Native American peoples. On many reservations of the Southwest you can visit some striking landmarks which are still held sacred. You can see traditional homes, such as pueblos and hogans. And sometimes you can watch traditional dances and ceremonies.

If you would like to learn more about the American Indians of the Southwest by visiting them, it is important to

The Zuni Olla Maidens at the Gallup Inter–Tribal Indian Ceremonial, Gallup, New Mexico.

know a few simple rules. Some tribes do not allow photography at all. Others may allow photography during some dances, but not during others. Often a fee to take pictures will be charged. When photographing, be sure to ask permission first. Do not run around and make loud noises, especially when attending a dance. And do not talk to the dancers. Many areas may be off-limits to visitors, so be sure to check with tribal officials before venturing out on your own.

The American Indians of the Southwest are proud of their tribal lands and their ceremonies, and they welcome visitors who come to enjoy the sights and activities. But keep in mind that when you visit a reservation, you are visiting someone's home, not a museum or theme park. Be respectful. ❖

Tablitas

Tablitas are often worn by Pueblo and Hopi girls and women during dances. Besides being very colorful, tablitas also feature some important designs. Stair steps, for instance, symbolize clouds. Made out of thin wood, many tablitas also feature feathers attached to the top.

Athabascan language: language spoken by the Navajo and Apache.

Blessingway: Navajo ceremony.

Cacique: pueblo village leader.

Changing Woman: deity among the Navajo and Apache.

Codetalker: Navajo soldiers in World War II.

Coronado, Francisco Vasquez de: Spanish conquistador who was the first European to visit the American Southwest.

Elder Brother: deity for the Tohono O'odham.

Field village: traditional village for the Tohono O'odham.

First Man: Navajo deity.

First Woman: Navajo deity.

Four Corners: an area which includes the corners of Utah, Arizona, Colorado and New Mexico.

Fourth World: the last of four worlds which the ancestors of the Pueblo and Hopi lived in.

Gathering of the clans: the traditional migration of all Hopi clans to the Hopi mesas in Arizona.

Hisatsinom: the Hopi name for their prehistoric ancestors.

Hogan: traditional, eight-sided Navajo home.

Holy People: Navajo deities.

Hopi Clown: character in many Hopi dances who makes fun of people.

Kachinas: helpful spirits among the Hopi who live for half the year in the Hopi villages and the other half atop the San Francisco Peaks.

Kikmongwi: village leader among the Hopi people.

Kino, Eusebio: Spanish father who traveled among the Tohono O'odham in the late 1600s.

Kiva: religious chamber that is often underground among

the Pueblo and Hopi peoples.

Long Walk: a forced march of the Navajo people in 1864 to eastern New Mexico.

Moieties: large community groups found among the eastern pueblos.

Nightway: Navajo ceremony.

Oraibi: the oldest Hopi village.

Pueblo Revolt: a successful uprising by the Pueblo peoples in 1680.

Ramada: a structure built by desert dwelling peoples to provide shade.

Reservation: a parcel of land set aside by the government for Indian tribes.

Saguaro cactus: a tall cactus which grows in southern Arizona and produces a red fruit each summer.

San Xavier Mission: a large white mission built by the Spanish south of Tucson.

Sipapu: the traditional Pueblo and Hopi place of emergence into this world.

Tablitas: headdresses worn by female Pueblo dancers.

Toka: a traditional game similar to field hockey that is played by Tohono O'odham and Pima girls and women.

Trading post: a store set up by Anglo-American traders among the Navajo people in the 1800s.

Waila: a type of music popular among the Tohono O'odham and Pima peoples.

Well Villages: a traditional village that the Tohono O'odham lived for part of the year.

Yucca: a common desert plant which many Indian peoples traditionally utilized.

Waila, also known as chicken scratch, is a type of music popular among the Tohono O'odham and Pima peoples.

INDEX

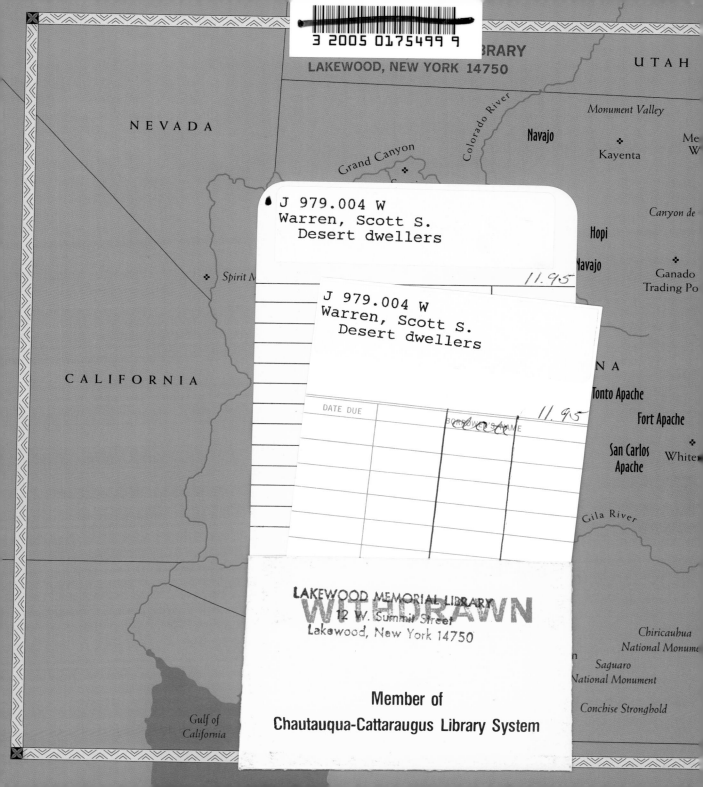